PUFFIN BOOK

TOM'S PRIVATE WAR

Robert Leeson was born in Cheshire in 1928. He served in the Army in the Middle East and worked abroad before returning to Britain, where he has been a journalist for over forty years. He is the author of sixty books for young people, as well as studies of industrial history and literary criticism for adults. In 1985 he was awarded the Eleanor Farjeon Award for services to children and literature. Robert Leeson is married with a son and daughter, and now lives in Hertfordshire.

Some other books by Robert Leeson

THE DOG WHO CHANGED THE WORLD

For younger readers

GERALDINE GETS LUCKY

NEVER KISS FROGS!

Tom's Private War

Robert Leeson

ILLUSTRATED BY
KENNY MCKENDRY

PUFFIN BOOKS

For Thomas

PUFFIN BOOKS

Published by the Penguin Group
Penguin Books Ltd, 27 Wrights Lane, London W8 5TZ, England
Penguin Books USA Inc., 375 Hudson Street, New York, New York 10014, USA
Penguin Books Australia Ltd, Ringwood, Victoria, Australia
Penguin Books Canada Ltd, 10 Alcorn Avenue, Toronto, Ontario, Canada M4V 3B2
Penguin Books (NZ) Ltd, 182–190 Wairau Road, Auckland 10, New Zealand

Penguin Books Ltd, Registered Offices: Harmondsworth, Middlesex, England

First published 1998
1 3 5 7 9 10 8 6 4 2

Text copyright © Robert Leeson, 1998
Illustrations copyright © Kenny McKendry, 1998
All rights reserved

The moral right of the author has been asserted

Filmset in Bembo

Made and printed in England by Clays Ltd, St Ives plc

British Library Cataloguing in Publication Data
A CIP catalogue record for this book is available from the British Library

ISBN 0–140–38427–8

1

TOM MET THE rest of the Orchard Road gang on the Meadows, as usual, that Saturday morning.

''Lo,' said Duggie. Molly grinned. William gave him a quick nod, then issued his orders.

'We'll go to Burley Wood, and do the jumps.' Without waiting for an answer, he set off down the path over the fields, outside Daneford.

Tom groaned to himself. In Burley Wood, the game was jumping across the stream, each leap getting bigger as the brook ran wider. Molly thought it a daft game and sat it out. Duggie did a few jumps then waded over, leaving Tom in unequal contest with William – usually landing short – in the water.

They walked in silence. The sun was hot, another scorcher, the last of a terrific summer. A smashing holiday was nearly over.

On Monday, Tom, Duggie and Molly started at the big school, three miles away, down the hill from Daneford, in Castlewick town. William had been there a year already. He was the expert. Nobody talked about school any more. William had said the last word on that subject.

Besides, something else was on their minds, something bigger, much bigger, but vague, like a cloud on the skyline.

They all knew this was the last weekend of peace. There was going to be a war. There was nothing else for it.

Tom felt a touch on his arm.

'What are you thinking about, Tommy?' asked Molly. 'The war?'

He made a face and nodded.

She nodded too, and put an arm round his shoulder. Ahead of them, William turned and glared.

'Get a move on, you lot. Last one in the wood's a sissie.'

He broke into a run down the slope. The others followed more slowly. Below them stretched open parkland. Beyond was Burley Wood, dark and green.

Then William pulled up so sharply the others almost ran into him.

'Look at that,' he yelled. 'Look at that!'

2

ACROSS THE LEVEL turf of the park a fence now stretched, rough posts and wire. Behind it lay a sea of green and brown, not grass but row on row of tents. Among them moved hundreds of men in brown shirts and trousers.

By the fence a man in full uniform barred the way, rifle slung over his shoulder. The gang stopped open-mouthed.

'Hey, mister,' said Duggie. 'Can't we get

through here any more?'

'Don't be a dope,' snapped William. ''Course we can't. The Army's taken over. Come on.' He took charge once more. 'We'll go down the Clough.'

That was more like it, thought Tom. The Clough was a steep slope running down from the edge of the Rec to the canal bank. It was dotted with gorse bushes and the game was rolling downhill without getting full of prickles. No winners, no losers.

The gang faced about and headed back towards Daneford.

'Hey,' said Duggie, jerking his thumb back towards the camp. 'Do they have to live in those bell tents all the time? It's murder. I slept two nights in one with the Scouts. Freezing cold, earwigs down your neck, beetles up your bum . . .'

'Dah!' jeered William. 'They won't be here long. They'll be off over to France. My dad reckons it'll last six months, no more. When the Allies gang up on Adolf – you'll see.'

'I don't know,' said Tom. 'My dad says that's what they thought in the Great War. And he was in France for four years.'

William was crushing. 'Well, your dad doesn't know anything about this war. My dad does. He's an air raid warden and he knows about all the secret weapons they've got.'

Tom stood his ground. 'My dad might be going in the Army again. He knows all about it.'

'Get off,' snorted William. 'He'll be too old.'

'They reckoned on the wireless,' put in Duggie, 'that all blokes'll have to go, right up to forty-one.'

Everyone was silent. Forty-one was old.

'They'll be taking women as well,' said Molly. 'I'm going to join the Land Army.'

'You never. You're not old enough,' came from William.

'I will be when I'm seventeen.'

'Come on,' said Tom. 'Let's get a move on before some other gang gets to the Clough.'

William didn't like anyone else giving orders. But the others were running already. He put on speed, passed them and ran on. Molly gave Tom a grin.

'Never happy unless he's in front,' she murmured out of the corner of her mouth.

Tom grinned back. Molly had her cousin sized up.

But William had stopped again, by the gateway to the Rec, waving for them to halt.

'Military objective, right ahead,' he shouted.

3

THE FAR CORNER of the Rec, beyond the football pitch and the swings, was ringed in with barbed wire, cutting off the way to the top of the Clough.

Inside the steel ring were more men in khaki, without jackets, sleeves rolled up. They were filling sandbags and building a wall round a deep, fresh-dug pit.

At the centre of the ring, grey steel barrel pointing skywards, was a gun, unlike anything

Tom had ever seen in the magazines about the Great War.

As the gang drew closer, a tall, sandy-haired soldier left the working party and came up to the barbed wire. He had a cheerful red face and blue eyes.

'Hey, mister,' said Tom. 'What's that gun?'

'Ack-ack, son.'

'What's ack-ack, mister?' asked Molly.

William turned on her. 'You are a dope. It's anti-aircraft.' He turned to the soldier. 'My dad's an air raid warden.'

'Oh ah.' The soldier gave William a strange look.

'Hey, mister,' put in Duggie. 'What are those things on your sleeves? Are you an officer?'

The soldier laughed. 'No, son. Those are my stripes. I'm a bombardier.'

'That's the same as a corporal,' put in William knowingly.

Tom wanted to say, 'My dad was a bombardier in the last war,' but he kept it to himself. He didn't want to start William off again.

In any case, William had taken command. 'Right, you lot. Get lined up. We'll go up to the Croft.'

He saluted the soldier and the gang was marched away, leaving him shaking his head.

The Croft was a field on the other side of Daneford, with an oak tree where the gang often gathered at weekends. From its branches you could see for miles.

No sooner had they all climbed into their favourite seats than Duggie pointed. The other three followed his outstretched finger in amazement.

On the distant western skyline, glinting in the afternoon sun, swinging on invisible cables, were huge grey elephant shapes, twenty or more in an enormous circle.

'Airships,' gasped Duggie.

'Nah,' corrected William. 'They're barrage balloons. They're supposed to stop German bombers getting through to Liverpool and the docks.'

'Do you think there's really going to be air raids?'

'There's forced to be,' said William. 'Liverpool's going to be bombed flat, my dad said. And I'll tell you what. All the kids from Liverpool are going to be taken away.'

'Get off,' said the others in disbelief.

'Honest. They call them "evacuees". They'll be bringing some here.'

The gang was silent. Tom looked across the sky at the swinging grey elephant shapes. Yes, there was going to be a real war and it was coming here.

What Tom didn't know was that his own private war was about to begin.

4

O N SUNDAY, AT quarter past eleven, the war started, officially. Tom wasn't impressed at first. There was just this tired old man's voice on the wireless.

His dad looked out of the window and whistled through his teeth, as he always did when he was working things out. His mum put her apron up to her eyes. Tom felt strange inside.

He forgot about the war for a while when

he tried on the sports gear and school cap
they'd just bought for him. He didn't have to
wear full school uniform, the family couldn't
afford it.

Then the war became real again. Tom took
his gas mask out of its brown cardboard box.
It was black, shaped like a pig's head, with
a round plastic snout. Dad helped him on
with it, fixing the straps at the back of his
head.

The rubber smell was powerful. The perspex window misted up and Tom felt he was choking.

'Breath in and out steadily,' Dad said in his ear. The panicky feeling died, but he still couldn't see anything.

Dad pulled the mask off his head and they rubbed soap on the inside of the eyepiece. Then Tom pulled it on again himself, and he could see and breathe easily.

'Hey, can I go over to Duggie's with it on?' he asked.

'You can not.' His mum sounded angry. 'It's not a toy. You keep it safe in case it's needed some time.'

'That's it,' his dad chuckled. 'Wait till Bert Harris comes round with his rattle, shouting "Gas! Gas! Take cover!"'

'Frank, you ought to know better than joke about it.' Now Mum was telling Dad off.

Dad shrugged. 'Well, if I can't joke about it, who can?'

'I expect Mr Harris is only doing his duty,' went on Mum.

'Oh ah,' said Dad. 'But I can't stand him marching round like Lord Muck in his tin hat, as though the Germans are coming already.'

'Their William's just as bad as his dad – always throwing his weight about.' Tom had his say.

'You mind your own business – and get ready for Sunday School.' His mum put a stop to the argument.

When Tom got back later that afternoon, Mum and his sisters were cutting up big lengths of black cloth, while Dad fitted it to the kitchen window.

'Hope there's going to be enough blackout stuff,' she said, handing up another piece. 'You can't get it for love nor money now. There's queues at the shops for everything.'

'Ah,' muttered Dad through the safety-pins between his teeth. 'Queenie Robertson got in a queue for hair-grips and found she'd signed on for the old age pension.'

'Trust her,' began Mum, then burst out laughing. 'You're pulling my leg.'

'Anything's possible these days,' answered Dad. 'There.' He climbed down from the window. 'That'll have to do. We'll find out tonight if it lets light through.'

5

TOM LAY AWAKE. His younger brother in the other bed had dropped off already, but he was too excited to sleep. He could hear Mum and Dad moving about in the kitchen, locking up for the night.

He slipped from the bed and peered out of the window. Outside it was pitch dark, like a cellar. No moon, no street lamps, just a faint glow from the works in the valley below.

A terrific rat-tat-tat on the front door made him jump.

'Who's that?' He heard his mum's voice from the kitchen.

'I'm just going,' his dad replied. Bolts squeaked at the door below. Tom almost crept back to bed but curiosity kept him at the window. Faint movements from across the street told him there were other nosey parkers.

Now Dad had the front door open, speaking briskly. 'Yes, Bert, what can I do for you?'

'Mr Taylor.' Mr Harris's voice was very formal. Tom could hear where William got his way of talking from. 'I must ask you to put that light out.'

'Whatever for, Bert?'

'There's a distinct beam from your front window.'

'A little glim,' replied Dad. 'That's just

possible. We'd barely enough blackout cloth.
Anyway, we're just off to bed. We'll fix it
tomorrow. Good night then.'

'Tomorrow is not good enough. If you
cannot adjust the curtain then the light must

be extinguished.' Mr Harris became even more formal.

'I suppose they can see it all the way to Berlin.' Dad was sarcastic now. 'And they can't see the light from the works furnaces, eh?'

'They are not my responsibility. This street is, Mr Taylor, and I am ordering you to put that light out.'

'Oh, you are. Well, let me tell you, Air Raid Warden Harris, if you want to make me, you can fetch Sergeant Collins up from the police station to do it. Now good night.'

'Mr Taylor.' William's dad began to sound desperate. 'Don't you know there's a war on?'

'You what?' Dad's voice was sharp. 'I know more about war than you ever will.'

Across the road, a window went up with a slam. Then Tom heard Widow Robertson's screech.

'You tell him, Frank. Ask him about all those torch batteries he's keeping under the counter in that shop of his, till the price goes up.'

Air Raid Warden Harris couldn't face action on two fronts.

'You think on, Frank Taylor. I'll come back and check that window tomorrow.'

'You're welcome,' said Dad caustically. 'And good night.'

There was no answer, only the sound of retreating footsteps and windows quietly closing. The night was black and silent as Tom sneaked back to bed.

He was chuckling to himself over the way his dad had put William's dad in his place. But further down in his mind he had a sneaking feeling this might not turn out to be so funny.

And he was right.

6

AFTER THE NIGHT'S excitement, Tom overslept. Or he would have done if his mother hadn't turned him out of bed. She made him eat his breakfast properly, though, and he just caught the school bus at the top of Orchard Road by the skin of his teeth.

It was full already, but Duggie had saved him a few inches of space to squash into at the front. As Tom climbed on board, there was silence, then someone further along the

29

bus started to whisper. By the time the bus was trundling down the hill, there were sniggers and chuckles.

Duggie nudged him. 'Hey, d'you hear that? It was all over the place this morning.'

'What was?'

'Who are you trying to kid? Your dad tearing a strip off William's last night.'

Tom sneaked a look behind him along the crowded seats of the bus, then turned round

just as quickly. William sat there, his face stony.

Oh no, thought Tom.

But last night's rumpus vanished from his mind as the bus rolled into Castlewick, and Duggie and he jumped down to join the long trail of kids trudging up the road to school. Both carried their bags over one shoulder and gas mask cases on string across the other. They wore their new caps on the back of

their heads, as the bigger lads did. When they came near the school gates they could twitch them down to the correct angle over their eyes.

On the opposite pavement walked a crocodile of girls, Molly among them. Tom would have liked to wave but didn't dare. From now on boys and girls were kept apart for lessons and in separate playgrounds. They had to wait until evening or the weekends to get together.

Behind him Tom could hear William's voice. There was some pushing and shoving going on among his classmates. Duggie nudged Tom.

'Let's get a move on. They leg the new lads over if they can get up close.'

They speeded up. Tom noticed that the whole column was marching faster as the new boys tried to keep out of range. The school gates came into view and the stride

became a trot. Finally they went through into the school yard at a gallop, to the derisive laughter of the older lads.

The morning passed. They were shunted from one room to another until they settled in their own form. But Tom's relief did not last more than a minute.

Their teacher, a huge man with a bullet head and short-cropped hair, marched in.

'Gas,' he bellowed. 'One, two, three.'

Tom reached under his desk for the cardboard box and scrabbled with the lid. In vain . . . it would not open.

'Six, seven, eight . . .'

Desperately, Tom turned the case round. The lid stayed shut.

'Nine, ten. That boy in the corner is dead.'

From round the classroom came honking noises as the other lads laughed inside their gas masks. The teacher loomed over Tom.

'Give it to me, lad.' There was a ripping sound. 'Some smart alec thought it a good idea to put sticky tape on this boy's gas mask case. That could be lethal, lethal!'

From the back of the class, a boy blew into his mask. The air escaped from the rubber rim with a farting sound.

'You,' yelled the master. 'Outside. Class! Masks off and away.'

For the rest of the day, till the joke palled, Tom was asked if he wanted to be buried or cremated. But it was bearable, and by the time Duggie and he were heading for the terminus, he could laugh at it himself.

As they boarded the bus for home, they saw William with his mates.

"Lo, William,' they called.

"Lo, Duggie,' answered William, deliberately. But he looked past Tom without a word.

7

THAT WEEKEND THE 'vaccies' arrived from Liverpool – a coachload of them, pale and miserable, clutching cardboard suitcases, name labels tied to their coats.

Tom's mum was sorry for them. She wanted to take in a boy or girl but the house was too crowded. Widow Robertson, though, was on her own. She took an evacuee and the whole street knew about it.

'It's a crying shame. Those snobs up Birch

Lane looked the poor jiggers up and down and picked out the cleanest ones. When it was all done this poor little chap was left.'

Poor little chap? He was the same age as Tom, but hard as nails, Tom could see that, with a face like a ferret, a sharp nose and red eyes. He came out into the street just as the gang met up. William, who seemed to be in a good mood again, winked and raised his voice.

'Yeah, you know where Liverpool is – that little place across the Mersey from New Brighton.'

The evacuee rose to the bait.

'It's on the map, any road, not like this dump. There's nothing here, no flicks, two shops, a load of fields and a bunch of useless cows.'

'Our cows aren't useless,' said William, loftily.

'What use are they?'

'They give good milk, that's what.'

The Liverpool lad stared in disbelief.

'Don't be gormless. You don't get milk from those mucky things. It comes clean in bottles, round our way.'

The gang burst into laughter, punching each other. Even Molly, who felt sorry for him, had to grin.

The pale face reddened. He picked on Tom, who was his own size.

'What are you laughing at?'

Tom choked, and said hastily: 'Nowt, mate.'

'It had better be nowt, kidder.' The evacuee's tone was menacing. He turned on his heels and went into Widow Robertson's entry.

William looked scornfully at Tom. 'Fancy letting a Scouser talk to you like that. You should've poked him one.'

'Oh, forget it,' said Molly hastily.

But William was not going to forget.

8

SOME JOKER — TOM never found out who — started a new craze at school. They sneaked up behind the victim and cut the string on their gas mask case, sending it down to the ground with a clatter, then disappearing into the crowd.

That morning they picked on Scouser — as the Liverpool lad was now known.

And who was there, just a yard away, trying to keep a straight face when Scouser's gas mask case fell down? It was Tom.

Scouser lunged forward: 'You did that, you rotten git.'

'I never,' protested Tom.

Scouser raised his fist. William appeared out of thin air.

'No scrapping where the teachers can see. Over by the lavs.'

Like magic a crowd had gathered. Scouser and Tom were swept across the yard to a corner, safe from prying eyes, and in no time a circle formed.

'Get on with it, do him!' urged William. Reluctantly Tom put up his fists. But Scouser was on the move already, and using a different rule book.

Lowering his head, he ran it full into Tom's stomach. As Tom doubled up, Scouser caught him a beauty on the nose with his fist.

Before Tom could lay a finger on his opponent, the whistles sounded. The crowd streamed away, Scouser triumphant among them.

'You were useless,' William told Tom, who was dabbing his injured nose. 'You have to get him one back. You can't let a Scouser do that to you.'

'How can I?' demanded Tom. 'He doesn't fight fair.'

'Well, we won't either.'

'How d'you mean?'

'You leave that to me,' said William mysteriously, and turned his back on Tom.

9

AY BY DAY after his clash with Scouser the sinking feeling grew in Tom's stomach. He wanted his own back, yet he couldn't start another fight just like that. How did he know what Scouser would do?

What made it worse was seeing the evacuee every day in the street or the school yard with his mates. He would call out cheerfully: 'How's your nose, kidder?'

Even worse, Duggie sniggered the first

time it happened, until Tom sent him a withering look.

But suddenly, Scouser stopped his needling. Maybe he had tired of it, since Tom pretended to ignore him.

On the other hand, maybe something else was on his mind. By Wednesday that impudent smirk had gone from the pale face.

'Hey,' said Duggie, 'what have you done to Scouser? He looks sick – sort of scared of you.'

It was a comforting thought, but Tom didn't believe it. Scouser didn't scare that easily. What was going on?

On Thursday Tom found out. William appeared on his doorstep after school. Without a 'Hello', he began. 'Right, it's all fixed, for Saturday.'

'What's fixed?' Tom was bewildered.

'Getting your own back on Scouser, you dope. I promised you, didn't I?'

'Ho-ow?' Tom was uneasy at the gleam in William's eye.

'The Caves. I challenged Scouser. You both go down in the Caves and the one who stays in longest, wins.'

Tom's heart dropped into his boots. No one went into the Caves. At the foot of the Clough, near the canal bank, was a dark tunnel leading to abandoned salt-mine workings. Years before, the earth had collapsed in the lower galleries, letting in canal water and closing the mines. But at ground level, deep inside the Clough, a small maze of dank tunnels was still open.

'You're mad,' gasped Tom. 'If we go in there we might never come out again.'

'Yeah,' said William with relish. 'You should've seen Scouser's face when I told him. But he couldn't back out. He'll be there

Saturday morning with his mates. So you get
your own back. OK?'

Friday evening came and another caller. It
was Molly.

She whispered, 'Got something to tell you,
Tommy.'

Tom called back into the kitchen, 'Just

going up the road, Mum. Won't be long.'

As they reached the street, Molly said, 'Listen Tommy. This Caves thing. William's trying to get you.'

'Me?' Tom's voice rose.

'Hey, be quiet. Yeah. After what happened last Sunday over the blackout. Your dad made a monkey out of his dad. William wants his own back. He couldn't care less about Scouser. It's you he's after.'

'Get away,' said Tom, but he knew Molly was right. William never gave up on a grudge.

'Look, Tommy. Why not tell Scouser it's quits? He's just as scared.'

'Can't do that.' Tom's mouth clamped shut on the words.

'Well, look.' Molly quietly passed Tom a slender metal object. 'Take my fountain pen torch I had last birthday. No one'll spot it, but it'll help you in the Caves.'

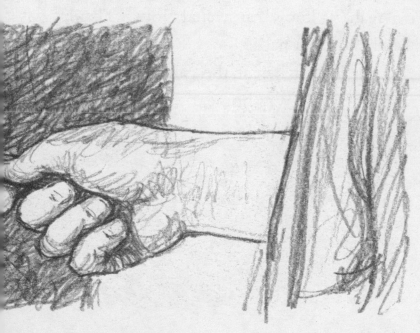

Tom shook his head. 'Can't do that, Molly. That'd be cheating.'

'Tom, don't be daft. If you fall down the borehole in the dark, what'll that be?' She nudged him and slipped the flashlight into his pocket.

Now they were in the top lane, Molly slipped her arm into Tom's.

'Look, William's my cousin, but he's so bossy I get fed up with him.'

'Yeah, I know,' answered Tom. 'Thanks, Molly, you're a pal.'

Later he left her at the gate of her house and ran all the way home.

10

WHEN TOM REACHED the canal bank on Saturday morning, Molly, Duggie and William were waiting, but no one else was in sight.

'Hey up,' he said. 'Maybe he's too scared to come.'

But just as he spoke, Scouser, white-faced and scowling, appeared round a bend in the towpath. Behind him were two mates, as tough-looking as he.

Scouser halted, pointing at the steep bank

of the Clough reaching high above them.

'Look at that. The tunnel's boarded up. We can't get in.'

Tom's spirits rose. Scouser was as scared as he was. And for another thing he was right. The opening to the mine workings was blocked with old railway sleepers.

But before he could say, carelessly, 'Well, that puts the tin lid on it,' William strode up to the bank, took hold of one of the timber baulks and jerked it aside. A dark slit opened in the green hillside and from it came a foul smell of cellars and drains.

'Got your gas mask, kidder,' joked one of the Liverpool lads. But neither Scouser nor Tom were laughing.

'We'll never get in there,' protested Scouser.

Faking boldness, Tom stepped forward. 'Want to give in, kidder?' he jeered.

'Up yours,' answered Scouser charmingly.

William raised a hand. 'Our man goes first. You follow. We keep time outside. After ten minutes we call you out. The one who gives up, or skrikes for help before that, is a sissie. OK?'

'OK!' Tom and Scouser spoke together.

'Now.' William spoke to Scouser's mates.

'Let's synchronize our watches.'

'What watches?' said one evacuee sarcastically, lifting his bare arm.

'OK, we'll manage on mine then,' answered William pompously – just like his dad. 'In you go, Taylor.'

Duggie moved up alongside Tom. 'I'll hold that other plank back – give him more room.' Then he whispered to Tom: 'Listen, mate. My brother says inside on the right, twenty yards, there's a side tunnel. Hide in there till he gives up. Good luck.'

'Thanks, Duggie,' Tom whispered back, and holding his breath tight, he thrust himself through the gap into the foul emptiness beyond.

11

WITH EVERY STEP Tom took the cleft narrowed, until he found himself gripped on both sides. All around was dark, pitch blackness, darker than any night, blacker than the blackout. It was as though the whole weight of the Clough was squeezing him, tighter and tighter.

A squealing sound burst on his ears. His heart leapt. Then he realized it was the sound of his own breath forcing its way out.

He drew in a great lungful, then regretted it. The stench of dead air, trapped under the earth for years, was horrible. Gritting his teeth, he took shallow breaths, one, two, three, and began to advance into the void. One breath, one step.

The rough sides of the passage, part soil, part rotting timber, plucked at him. The air was harsh in his throat. But he had to go on. Breath, pace, breath, pace.

Twenty. His right arm shot into space. Duggie's brother was right. There was a side vent. Carefully he turned right, twisted his body round, backing into the opening.

It was all by touch – he could hear nothing, see nothing. He began to feel dizzy. Lights flashed in his eyes.

He'd stopped breathing. His chest felt as if it would burst. Start again, in, out, one, two.

William had said ten minutes. Ten minutes

was ten times sixty seconds, six hundred altogether. He would count to six hundred and then go out. They couldn't crib at that.

As he reached fifty, a sound from the tunnel beyond his hiding place shook him – a slithering sound like a snake, a giant snake. It came closer. Tom went rigid, his skin crawling.

Then, from the darkness, only a few feet away, came a ripe Liverpudlian oath. Tom choked on a hysterical laugh. It was Scouser. If he reached out from his hiding place, he could touch him as he went past. But Tom kept still, hardly breathing. If he was going to win this dare, Scouser had to believe that Tom had gone further in, where he daren't follow.

Suddenly light flashed on the roof of the outer passage. Scouser had a torch! He was cheating. He was even more scared than Tom.

For a second the light swung into the side gallery. Tom ducked but the beam wavered back. Then it vanished as Scouser pressed on into the darkness.

As he went he muttered. 'I won't . . . give up. I won't let those . . . Danefords . . . beat me.'

The sound died away. Tom's sides ached with silent laughter, his chest with held breath, his head with relief.

12

TOM'S BODY GAVE a great jump. His mind had gone blank. He had fallen asleep? Maybe he was dreaming. He wasn't in this dark foul-smelling hole under the earth. He was in his bed at home and soon he'd wake up.

He put out a hand. He could feel the soft slimy soil of the walls, the chill creeping up his legs. He was in the Caves. And so was Scouser, somewhere in the darkness.

How long? He'd lost count. He thought

quickly. Say two hundred. He began again. Two hundred and one, two hundred and two. No, that was too slow. One two, three . . .

The voice in his mind chanted monotonously and his thoughts wandered again. Did blokes used to work down below, under the canal, with their lanterns, chopping at the rock salt, all day, every day? Were they down here when the water burst in? Did they drown?

Ninety-nine. He came back to reality. Was that three hundred or four hundred? He tried to concentrate but the numbers hypnotized him. He beat on his leg with one hand – forty-six, forty-seven . . .

At last he could stand it no longer. It was six hundred seconds – ten minutes. Time was up. It had to be. His legs were so stiff they hurt as he lurched forward, hands waving in front of him.

In the main cutting he halted. There was not a sound from Scouser, wherever he was, not a gleam from that cheating torch.

A stray thought struck him. Maybe Scouser had sneaked back to the open air. If so, I've won. The notion gave him fresh strength, and he pushed boldly ahead till the closing walls told him he was at the entrance.

He could see the opening now. Thrusting and wriggling, he tumbled out into the daylight, the brightness hurting his eyes.

He gazed around him. No one there. They'd gone, the rotten lot. No, wait a bit. He could hear voices, laughter. They were having a giggle about him.

The sounds came from behind a bush some ten yards away. Dropping to his knees, Tom crawled up to it. Then raising his head, he heard a clicking sound. Someone was playing cobs.

He sprang up, ready to tell them what he

thought of the lot of them, then ducked down again. There were five there – William, Molly, Duggie and two Liverpool lads. No Scouser.

Molly spoke. 'William. We ought to look for them. It's well gone ten minutes. I counted.'

'Get away.' William spoke carelessly.

'Nowhere near. Let's have another game. OK, kidder?'

A spasm of anger shook Tom. William had set this up. He didn't give a toss, though, what happened to Scouser or to him.

Then came a spasm of alarm. If Scouser were still down there in the Caves, the Liverpool lad had won. Wait a bit, though. No one up here knew that and neither did Scouser. He could sneak back inside, hide in the side tunnel and wait for Scouser to give up.

Then came a spasm of deeper alarm. Real fear. Suppose Scouser hadn't come out because something had gone wrong.

Turning and clenching his teeth, Tom fought his way back, past the timbers, into the dark tunnel once more.

13

TOM BURST THROUGH into the wider space beyond the entrance, ran, tripped, fell. The earth was slimy. Spitting, he struggled up and on. Where was the side turning? He'd forgotten to count and he was past it already.

Dope! He'd forgotten something else. He had Molly's torch. Fumbling, fingers greasy with mud, he fished it from his pocket and pressed the switch.

A narrow jet of light made the roof glisten.

Then it showed up the darker darkness of his
hiding place. He plunged in, waving the
flashlight ahead of him.

There was no way through, just a cave-like
space. Back to the main tunnel he went, and
pressed on. Darkness and silence wrapped
around him.

'Scouser!' he yelled. His voice died in the

great emptiness. 'Scouser! You there?' He tried again. 'It's well gone ten minutes!'

No answer. That was wrong. He had to be there. A sudden terrible thought stopped Tom's rush. Maybe the Liverpool lad didn't know about the lower galleries, or the shaft that led down to them. Maybe he'd fallen . . .

The tiny torch beam circled the ground, then the roof. Nothing. Nothing.

'Scouser!' The sound echoed back to Tom as he moved into a much larger space.

The earth beneath him crumbled. He slipped and slid. Then his knees jarred against something solid. The torch clashed on metal.

Soil and stones loosened by his feet flew away. Heart in mouth, he heard them splash into water far below.

The torch went out. The bulb must have broken when it hit the iron rails. Fearfully Tom reached out and felt a grid shape in front of him. Then his hand slipped into nothingness. There was a hole in the grating.

Scouser had fallen through.

For seconds he clung to the iron grille, then slowly he forced himself to go back the way he had come. He had to get help.

Even as he turned he felt something touch his shoulder and his neck. With a half scream he swung and struck out with all his might.

14

HIS FIST HIT something hard and soft in one. A light shone in his eyes. A voice cried out in pain.

'Aaargh! Me nose!'

'Scouser!' yelled Tom, in relief. 'Where have you been? I thought you'd fallen down the borehole.'

'I thought *you* had,' came the amazed reply. 'I've been looking for you.'

'Get away.' Tom started to laugh. 'How's your nose?'

'How d'you think, kidder? You got your own back, eh?'

'Yeah,' said Tom. 'It's a draw.' Then he remembered. 'You know, I thought you'd gone out so I went to look. That lot out there are playing cobs. We could have drowned for all they cared.'

'Right, mate. But you came back to look for me?' Scouser sounded incredulous.

'Course I did,' said Tom. 'I mean, you

wouldn't have been down here if we hadn't
. . . 'Then he had another thought. 'Where
were you hiding?'

Scouser grabbed him by the arm. 'Come
on, kidder, I'll show you. There's another
hole.'

'There's lots.'

'This is different. Come on.' He dragged
Tom behind him, his torch beam lighting the
way. They were in another, narrower, passage.

Tom could feel the ground sloping below his
feet.

'Hey! It's going up.'

'Too true, mate, and look up there.'

Far above their heads, at the top of a kind
of chimney, was daylight.

'Another way out,' shouted Tom, excited.

'Yeah, and you know what? We go out that way and they'll think we're still under here. What d'you reckon?'

'Smashing!' Then Tom stopped. 'How do we get up, though? It's too high.'

'We do like the steeplejacks. Put your back on one side and your feet on the other and walk up. Watch.

As Tom stared he saw, by the faint light above, Scouser, body bent double, working his way up the chimney. Soon his climbing form blocked out the day.

'Come on,' his muffled voice commanded. Tom followed, heaving and straining with back and feet, spitting out the dirt that Scouser's boots showered on him.

Tom's whole body ached but he did not dare relax his knees. If he lost his grip he'd shoot right down into the tunnel again. Instead he pushed with all his might, shoulders, elbows, heels and toes.

'Here we are, kidder,' called Scouser.

Panting, they struggled out of the narrow opening into full daylight, blinking in the sun. Bushes blocked their way, but they shoved them to one side and stood up straight.

To look full into the muzzle of a rifle.

15

BEHIND THE GUN barrel loomed the sunburnt face and broad shoulders of a man in uniform.

As Tom and Scouser shot their hands into the air he burst into laughter.

'Stone the crows. A couple of kids.' He shouted over his shoulder. 'Hey, Corp!'

Tom and Scouser lowered their arms and gazed about them. They had climbed out at the top of the Clough, bang in the middle of the ack-ack emplacement. In front of them the grey gun barrel reached skywards, ringed in with neat rows of sandbags.

Further off, by the barbed wire, a fire was blazing. Two men in khaki were busy with a kettle. One turned and strode towards them. Tom recognized him by the two stripes on his sleeves.

'How did you two get in here?'

'Climbed up the pipe, mister. Hey, that's a smashing cannon. What sort is it?'

'Shouldn't really tell you, son,' said the bombardier sternly. But his eyes smiled. 'Still, Adolf knows all about these guns already. It's a Bofors 40 millimetre.'

Tom stared at the soldier's cap with its worn polished badge. He read the word 'Ubique'.

'Hey, my dad's got a badge like that,' he gasped. 'He was a bombardier in the last war.'

'Was he? I bet he saw some action,' the soldier said.

Scouser broke in. 'Not much action this time, eh, mister? Nothing happening.'

The bombardier looked serious. 'Don't kid yourself, son. This war's going to warm up before long.'

He pointed towards the gate in the barbed wire. 'And you two had better hop it before my battery commander comes. We'll be test-firing the gun soon. Hey, and don't come up the chimney again. That way's *verboten*.'

'OK!' Tom and Scouser spoke together. At the gate they turned and gave the thumbs-up sign.

Turning back, they stared into the baffled, angry face of William.

16

BEHIND WILLIAM STOOD Molly and Duggie, grinning with relief, and behind them Scouser's mates, open-mouthed.

'How did you get here?' demanded William. 'We've been looking all over the shop for you. We nearly went to the police.'

His voice stirred Tom's anger, which had been building up all week.

'Who are you trying to kid? You lot were playing cobs while Scouser and me were stuck down in the Caves.'

'Down in the Caves? You never. You both sneaked off out.'

Scouser stepped forward so aggressively that William moved back. He pointed to the mud on his jacket and Tom's.

'If we weren't down there, what's this stuff? Scotch mist?'

The others laughed, heating William up even more.

'Well, if you were in the Caves, how come you're up here now?' he asked furiously.

'That's a military secret,' answered Tom scornfully. 'Take no notice of him, Scouser.'

'You're finished in this gang,' William told Tom.

'No, he's not,' Molly spoke from behind William. 'He's still in, and so's Scouser if he wants, and his mates.'

'Who says?'

'I say,' piped up Duggie.

Scouser put his arm over Tom's shoulder. 'Come on, kidder,' he said. The gang, now enlarged, strolled towards home. William, after a pause to sulk, trailed after them.

Tom felt a warm glow spread inside him. Everything had turned out OK, after all.

But it hadn't.

17

JUST AS THE procession reached Tom's street it ran into an ambush. Widow Robertson, arms folded, stood in their path.

'Where have you been?' she demanded of Scouser. She stared. 'And all that filth on your windcheater.'

She turned on Tom. 'It's your fault. Taking him down one of your mucky places in his clean clothes.'

She raised her voice and the street rang.

'Wait till I tell your father.'

At these words, the little crowd split up like magic, each heading in a different direction. Tom was suddenly on his own.

With Widow Robertson's words in his ears, he crept up the garden path to his kitchen door.

But Tom's luck had not run out. Just as his unwilling foot was on the doorstep, a strange sound filled the air. It was a great wavering musical howl, rising and falling.

Dad appeared in the kitchen with Tom's little brother by the hand and carrying three gas mask cases.

'About turn, son. Down to the shelter. That's the air-raid siren.'

Outside, now, the street was full of people, not hurrying but moving purposefully, smiling and joking, calling to one another.

Tom remembered the bombardier's words:

'It's going to warm up soon.' Was this it? Was
Daneford going to be bombed flat?

At the top of the shelter steps stood
William's dad, in a dark greatcoat and steel
helmet.

'Take your places, please,' he called. 'There
is no need to be alarmed. Everything is under
control.'

The underground chamber was cold and

damp. It smelt of earth, and Tom was suddenly reminded of the Caves. Lights came on as people shuffled along the narrow benches, making room for each other.

Tom saw Molly on the seat opposite. She winked at him. He handed over her torch and whispered: 'The bulb went in the caves, sorry.'

She grinned. 'Forget it. It was worth it. The look on William's face, when he saw you and Scouser with those soldiers!'

As the shelter filled up, William's dad called, 'Everyone in now. The doors can be closed. Nothing to worry about. This may well be a false alarm.'

Just as he spoke there was a distant thud. The lights dimmed and a baby wailed. Someone called, 'Oh, they're dropping bombs.'

'No, no, love,' said Tom's dad. 'That's not a bomb. It's a gun, maybe that one at the Rec.'

As he spoke there came another 'crump'. William's dad spoke, importantly. 'That sounds too big for a gun.'

'It's a new sort of gun,' burst out Tom. 'A Bofors 40 millimetre. They're test-firing it.'

In the silence, everyone looked, amazed, at Tom. Dad grinned.

Then, as Tom swelled with pride, his mother said, 'Tom, what's that dirt on your sleeve?'

Tom gulped. But across the shelter, Widow

Robertson spoke soothingly. 'Oh, he probably picked it up in the shelter. Mucky places. My boy's got some on his windcheater.'

She patted Scouser's head. He made a face. Then she went on: 'I expect it'll all come out in the wash.'

Further along the benches, someone began to sing:

> *'We're going to hang out the washing*
>   *on the Siegfried Line,*
> *Have you any dirty washing, Mother dear?'*

As the singing filled the shelter, from outside came another, louder sound, like the air-raid warning, but on one steady note.

'The all-clear, ladies and gentlemen,' said William's dad, getting in the last word.